STEVE HUTCHISON
CREEPYPASTA DREAMS

STEVE HUTCHISON

CREEPYPASTA
DREAMS

First Printing: 2023
ISBN-13: 9781998881574

Bookstores and wholesalers: Please contact books@terror.ca.

Tales of Terror
tales@terror.ca
www.terror.ca

Enter the realm of the unknown with Creepypasta Dreams. This spine-chilling collection features 50 haunting tales that blur the line between reality and your deepest fears.

Immerse yourself in a world of strange creatures and sinister irony, where each story is guaranteed to leave you breathless with fear.

As you delve into it, ask yourself: are you the one reading the book, or is the book reading you?

STORIES

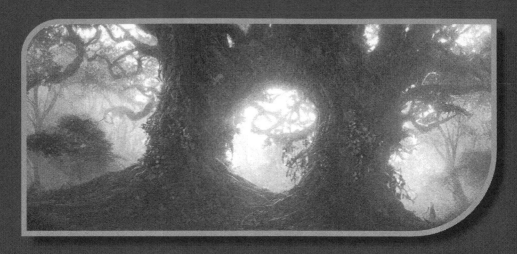

CANCER TREE

Jenna and Michelle were desperate to save their father from the cancer that was slowly taking over his body. They had heard rumors of a mysterious tree deep in the forest, whose fruits were said to have the power to cure any illness. Determined to try anything to save their father, the sisters set out into the forest to find the tree.

Week after week, they brought back more and more fruits from the tree, feeding them to their father in the hopes that they would save him. And to their amazement, their father's condition began to improve. His cancer was in remission, and the sisters were overjoyed.

But their father's relief was short-lived. As he continued to eat the fruits from the mysterious tree, he became increasingly distant and mentally absent. His eyes grew darker, and he began to have nightmares about the tree, describing it in detail even though he had never seen it. His language gradually changed, and soon his daughters could no longer understand him when he spoke.

Eventually, their father stopped talking altogether, and the sisters grew increasingly worried. One day, they found vines growing from his legs, and his skin began to resemble the bark of the tree. He woke up one morning, his body entirely covered in bark.

Realizing the connection between their father's condition and the tree, the sisters brought gasoline to the tree and set it on fire. But when they returned to their father's house, they found him burned to death. His cancer was gone, but so was he. The sisters were left with nothing but regret and sorrow, as they realized that the price of their father's cure was his very soul.

THE POTION

As I ventured deeper into the woods, the sunlight filtering through the trees began to fade. I started feeling cold, but I pushed on, driven by my curiosity.

And then, I stumbled upon it. A small, intricately carved wooden box. My fingers trembled as I unlatched and lifted the lid. Inside, I found a tiny woman, no more than 6 inches tall. Her eyes were filled with a desperate plea, and she begged me to gather the ingredients for a magic potion that would allow her to return to her original size.

Without hesitation, I agreed to help her. She gave me a list of seven ingredients, each more elusive than the last, scattered throughout the city. I set off on my quest, my mind consumed with thoughts of the small woman and her plight.

Days turned into weeks, and I searched high and low for the ingredients. Some were easy to find, while others proved to be more difficult. But I was determined to help the small woman, and I would not give up.

Finally, I had gathered all seven ingredients. I approached the small woman with the potion in hand, and she eagerly drank it down.

But as she began to grow, her true face was revealed. A cackle of maniacal laughter escaped her lips as she blew powder on my face. I stumbled backward, my vision blurring. When it cleared, I realized with horror that I had shrunk. I was trapped in a world of giants, and the small woman, now towering above me, was mocking me.

Ten years have passed since that fateful day, and I am still trapped in this wooden box. The small woman's laughter still echoes in my mind, taunting me with the knowledge that I will never escape. I am forever doomed to be her prisoner, a tiny, helpless pawn in her twisted game.

THE IMPOSSIBLE HOUSE

The house at the end of the dead-end street was a strange and addictive attraction for Brian. Every weekend, he would visit the house, sometimes even introducing new people to it. But one day, when no one wanted to go with him, Brian decided to explore the house alone.

As he opened the front door, the first room was always different, and this time it had a set of spiral stairs leading up or down. The experience was different and scarier alone. He explored several rooms before getting locked in one with a hole in the ground. Brian threw a coin in the hole and never heard a sound. He tried to find a way out but couldn't. He spent four days trapped before he decided to jump.

But when he jumped, he fell and fell, until it felt like he was floating and eventually he fell asleep. When he woke up, he was back in his bedroom, confused about his dream. He couldn't believe that everything he had experienced in the house was just a dream. But as he got out of bed, he noticed that his clothes were wet and his hair was matted with seaweed. Something was not right.

He opened his wardrobe doors, and there, in front of
him, was a portal. It was a swirling vortex of light and
it sucked him in. The next thing he knew, he was in a
body of water, and he could feel the weight of the water
pulling him down. He tried to swim to the surface but it
was too far away. Was he moving at all or was the surface
moving? His lungs ached for air, but he couldn't reach
the surface. Eventually, he realized he was drowning.

Brian saw his own funeral and his loved ones for the last
time. But when they lowered him into his grave, the lights
went out, and he was trapped there for six days. He finally
broke free and crawled to the surface, but the surface was a
basement with a dirt floor. The room was so big he couldn't
see the walls. He ran and ran, but never reached a wall.
Brian spent eternity exploring the impossible house he loved
so much. A house that was a puzzle, where nothing made
sense, and he was trapped in it forever, a prisoner of its
twisted halls, doomed to wander its endless maze forever.

FATE

Brad and Patrick were two cerebral mathematicians who were obsessed with the concept of fate. They spent their days devising intellectual games, games that could be played without tokens, cards, or miniatures; games that were played with memory, perception, and luck. Their favorite game was called "Fate" and they believed that by playing this game, they could control their destiny.

The game would begin with one player approaching the nearest stranger and asking for their name. If the stranger gave out their name, the player would then approach the nearest woman and ask her the same question. If the stranger refused to give their name, the player would approach the nearest man and ask him his name, and so on. The first player to get five names would call the other to claim victory.

Brad and Patrick had been playing this game for years, and they felt that they had perfected it. They had never lost a round. But on a stormy night, Patrick was struck by lightning while playing the game. His death was a shock to Brad, and he couldn't understand how this could have happened. He had always believed that their games were a way to control fate.

In the days following Patrick's death, Brad became increasingly fixated on the game. He thought that if he could just play the game one more time, he could change the outcome. So, he went back to playing "Fate" alone. However, as he was about to ask the first man his name, lightning struck him, and Brad saw the man collapse to the ground. The man died immediately, and Brad understood something was terribly wrong. Despite his reluctance, he decided to test the game again on another stranger, who also met the same fate.

From that moment on, Brad stopped asking people their names. He would avoid strangers altogether. Occasionally, he would make a mistake and ask someone their name, and they would be struck by lightning, even inside their house. The game was not the game he thought it was, but it was called "Fate" for a reason.

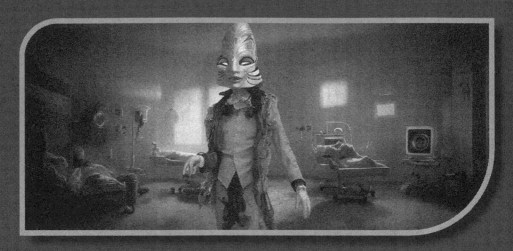

EERIE

The legend of Eerie, the cross-dimensional woman with a head of stone and cabal symbols carved, spread throughout the city like wildfire. People whispered about her, about how she traveled through television signals and claimed the souls of unsuspecting victims, trapping them inside their favorite movies for eternity. But Eerie wasn't just any ordinary being, she was the embodiment of retribution. She sought out those who had wronged others and made them pay for their sins most terrifyingly and tragically possible.

One day, an old man named Frank, who had made a living scamming innocent people out of their money, was visited by Eerie in his hospital room. Frank was suffering from Alzheimer's disease, and his mind was a foggy mess of confusion and memory loss. But Eerie saw right through him and knew that his soul was ripe for the taking.

"I am an angel of punishment," Eerie said, her voice as cold as death. "I have come to collect your soul and make you pay for your crimes. But first, I must know your favorite movie."

Frank, confused and terrified, struggled to remember the name of any movie he had ever seen. Eerie came back every week, asking the same question, but Frank could never remember the name of his favorite film. But Eerie was patient, and she knew that Frank's mind would eventually reveal the movie that held the key to his downfall.

One day, Eerie returned to the hospital room and asked Frank one more time. Frank, still confused, pointed to the television. On the screen was "Horror Night", a horror movie about a con man haunted by the ghosts of the people he had scammed.

Eerie trapped him inside the movie for eternity. Frank, unable to escape the horrors of his own past, would spend the rest of his days reliving his crimes over and over again, haunted by the very people he had wronged, as if the movie had been made only for him.

And so, the legend of Eerie lives on, a warning to all those who would dare to play with the souls of others. For Eerie will always be watching, waiting for her next victim to make their favorite movie choice.

COWBORG

Aaron had always been fascinated by the Wild West and had heard rumors of an abandoned town deep in the desert that was said to be haunted by a ghostly cowboy. Determined to uncover the truth, he set out on a journey with his camera in hand. As he traveled deeper into the desert, he became increasingly convinced that he was on the right track.

He came across a rundown ranch and as he approached, he saw a figure standing in the doorway - a cowboy unlike any he had ever seen before. The cowboy was a cyborg, with an iron jaw and a gun in his hand. He identified himself as Cowborg, the guardian of the abandoned Wild West town. He warned Aaron not to enter the town, stating that he would shoot any trespasser who attempted to enter.

Despite the warning, Aaron continued to approach Cowborg and the town. As a result, he was met with a bullet from Cowborg's gun and fainted, collapsing on the ground. When he woke up, he found himself in the same town, but in the year 1888. The town looked like all Western towns, but he recognized technology from his time.

The town was bustling with life, but as he looked closer, Aaron realized that the people were all ghosts, trapped in an eternal cycle of death and despair. The ghostly cowboy, Cowborg, was the town's executioner, and it was his job to keep the spirits of the dead trapped in the town forever.

CHRISTMAS SPIRIT

Bobby, a skeptical 13-year-old, had always harbored doubts about the mall Santa's authenticity. He had always believed that the mall Santa was just some man in a suit, and not the real Santa Claus. So, one day, Bobby decided to put his theory to the test. He went to the mall, determined to catch the mall Santa in some sort of deception.

Bobby followed the mall Santa through the crowded mall, taking pictures of him with his phone, hoping to catch him in the act. He observed the mall Santa as he talked to children and gave out candy canes, but still found no proof that he was a fraud.

But his investigation took a darker turn when the mall Santa disappeared into the service corridor. Bobby followed him, determined to find out what he was hiding. He followed the mall Santa through the winding corridors, taking pictures and recording videos with his phone, but still found nothing out of the ordinary.

The mall Santa vanished into the men's room. Bobby waited outside for 10 minutes, but the mall Santa never emerged. Bobby ventured inside, scanning the stalls for any sign of the elusive Santa, but found nothing. He even looked under the stalls and in the trash cans, but still nothing.

Confused and frightened, Bobby decided to leave the mall and take the bus home. But when he got there, he couldn't find his phone. He searched through his pockets and backpack, but it was nowhere to be found. He retraced his steps, but still nothing.

It was Christmas Eve and Bobby was still thinking about his phone and the mall Santa. When he grabbed his last Christmas present, his parents didn't recognize the wrapping paper and couldn't remember any gift that was that shape. Bobby opened it and, confused, found his phone inside. The phone suddenly rang and he recognized his ringtone. The caller's name on the screen read "Santa".

Bobby was terrified. He didn't know how Santa had gotten his phone or why he was calling him. He didn't pick up the phone and never saw Santa again, but he couldn't shake the feeling that the mall Santa was somehow involved. He had always been skeptical of the mall Santa, but now he was convinced that there was something truly dangerous about him. Bobby never forgot that strange experience and always kept an eye out for the mall Santa, never quite sure if it was the real deal or something far more sinister.

FRANCO THE FROG

Philip, a young man, starts noticing stickers of the cartoon character Franco the Frog all over the city. He remembers the violent cartoon frog from trading cards he used to collect, but for some reason, no one he mentions the sticker to remembers them.

One day, as he sits on the toilet in the public washroom of his school, he sees a Franco the Frog sticker behind the door. This one has a prompt written below it: "Walk and only turn right until you find me." Without thinking, Philip followed the directive and walked in the school halls, only turning right when he had the option. He ended up in a hallway with only a door at the end. On the door was a Franco the Frog sticker with a message written on it: "Go down until you no longer can."

Philip followed three more stickers until he had no idea where he was. The basement was cold and moist. It stank. As he turned the corner, he was horrified to see Franco the Frog, large and taller than a human, come out from behind a boiler. It was a giant, grotesque cartoon character. Franco the Frog told Philip that he had been watching him and that he "likes his style." Franco pointed to a small door behind a metal stairway and invited Philip to come to meet his family and have dinner.

Philip was confused and paralyzed by fear. It took him a while to answer and he said "I have to go to class." He wasn't sure why he answered that. Philip felt hypnotized by Franco and followed him to the small door. Before dialing the secret combination on the lock, Franco made sure Philip couldn't see. Franco unlocked the door and gently dragged Philip inside.

Philip blacked out and woke up tied to a dinner table with Franco's family around the table, all different revolting human-size animals.

Instead of praying or saying grace, the maniacal cartoons sang a joyful tune about the pleasures of dining and oral hygiene. As they began to feast on Philip's flesh, he realized that in this twisted world, there was no pain. Despite the horrors he was enduring, his body felt nothing as Franco and his twisted family carved into his limbs. The only things that ached were his heart and his soul.

CUBE HEAD

There was a woman who lurked in the shadows of the suburban streets; a creature unlike any other. Her head was shaped like a cube, cold and emotionless. The townsfolk never saw her during daylight hours, only when the night was at its darkest and the crickets sang their eerie songs.

She had a sinister reputation, known for stalking the neighborhood's pets, slipping into backyards, and snatching cats and dogs to take back to her hidden, sinister lair. No one knew why she did this, but tales of her twisted behavior spread like wildfire through the community.

One night, a group of friends decided to uncover the truth about the woman. They armed themselves with flashlights and cameras, and waited in a backyard known to be one of her favorite hunting grounds.

As the clock struck midnight, the woman appeared from the darkness. Her movements were jerky and unnatural, her cube-shaped head scanning the area for her next victim. She wore a white bathrobe and was barefoot. The friends were paralyzed with fear, unable to move as the woman closed in on them.

But one of them mustered the courage to take a photograph of her, capturing her flat, grotesque face forever. Her eyes were wild, and her mouth hung open in a silent scream.

They never saw the woman again, but the image of her cubic head still haunts them to this day. It is said that she still stalks the streets at night, searching for her next victim. If you hear strange noises outside your window or find your pet missing, be sure to lock your doors tight and pray that the woman with the cube head doesn't come for you next.

NIGHT DELIVERY

In the small town, a tale of terror circulated amongst its teenage residents - the legend of the Night Delivery. It was said that by dialing a mysterious phone number, one could have their deepest desires granted, but at what gruesome price?

Liam and Noah, two fearless gamers, became fascinated by the legend and dared to uncover the truth. Their quest led them to the elusive phone number, which they hesitantly dialed at the stroke of midnight. The legend instructed to speak the words "Please deliver" followed by a wish, and hang up.

With bated breath, Noah spoke his request first, seeking his coveted video game "Hot and Cold." As soon as he hung up, the doorbell rang, and to their horror, a copy of the game lay waiting for them on their porch, with no delivery person in sight.

The next day, Liam made his own request for a pair of running shoes. To their amazement, the shoes were delivered to their doorstep. The two boys became addicted to the Night Delivery and couldn't resist the temptation to call again.

But the third night proved to be fatal for Noah. Alone that night, as he reached for the phone, it rang of its own accord, and when he answered, the chilling words "Please deliver a healthy heart" echoed through the receiver. Noah's heart began to race, and with a deafening ring of the doorbell, it was ripped from his chest and delivered to the caller.

The town was left in mourning, and rumors of the Night Delivery's dark magic spread, warning others to steer clear of its evil influence. Yet, there were still those who dared to call, risking their own lives for a glimpse of their desires. The Night Delivery remains a cautionary tale, reminding all who hear it of the dangerous consequences of greed.

FUN

Andrea and Emma, 15 years old, decided to go to an unpopular amusement park one day without telling their parents. It was a weekend, but the amusement park was almost empty. The girls had heard rumors that the park was inferior and unsafe, but they didn't believe it. They wanted to see for themselves.

As they walked around the park, they noticed that it was indeed dirty and run-down. The rides looked old and rickety, and the staff seemed uninterested in their safety. But the girls were determined to have a good time.

As they were waiting in line for a ride, Andrea went to the washroom. Emma waited outside for her friend. When Andrea came out, Emma was nowhere to be found. Andrea heard a scream and saw, in the distance, a teddy bear mascot carrying Emma on its shoulder. Andrea panicked and ran after the mascot, determined to rescue her friend.

She followed the mascot to the haunted house attraction.
It was a labyrinth with doors opening and closing
mechanically. Andrea spend a good half-hour looking
for the mascot and her friend. She finally arrived in a
room with teenagers locked in cages, including Emma,
who was terrorized. Andrea went looking for the cage
keys but heard muffled voices in an adjacent room.

It was a big scary room with a dozen mascots, including the
teddy bear mascot. Andrea hit the teddy bear mascot and its
head fell. To her horror, there was no human inside. The doors
of this room closed themselves with a big bang, as the mascots
slowly walked toward Andrea who was too paralyzed to react.

SWIMMING LESSON

The sun beat down mercilessly on the group of friends as they arrived at the lake. Benjamin, Lucas, Tiffany, and Jade had been inseparable for years, but tensions were high between Benjamin and Lucas due to their shared history with Tiffany. Despite this, they all decided to put their differences aside and enjoy the day.

As they were swimming in the shallow water, Lucas suggested they both swim from the beach to the island located in the middle of the lake. Benjamin, hesitant at first, eventually agreed, eager to prove himself to his friends. However, little did Benjamin know that Lucas was an athlete swimmer and had ulterior motives. As they swam halfway to the island, Lucas started swimming increasingly fast and Benjamin tried to keep up, but eventually, he couldn't follow him anymore.

Desperate for air and out of energy, Benjamin started sinking into the depths of the lake, his screams for help going unheard. Tiffany watched in horror as her beloved Benjamin drowned before her eyes, tears streaming down her face as she blamed Lucas for his death. But Lucas refused to take responsibility for his actions, his heart hardened by jealousy and resentment.

A week later, around midnight, Lucas was alone at the public swimming pool. He loved to practice his swimming then because he didn't have to share the pool. But as he dove into the water, he could swear something brushed against his hand and when he came out of the water, he realized his championship ring was gone. He searched for it at the bottom of the pool and saw it on the pool drain.

In a moment of desperation, he reached for the ring, but as his fingers closed around it, a hand shot out of the drain and grabbed his, dragging him down into the depths of the pool. Lucas recognized Benjamin's tattoos on the arm and knew it was his ghost seeking revenge for his untimely death. Lucas couldn't free himself, ran out of breath, and drowned.

In the end, Lucas's obsession with winning led to his downfall as the very thing that gave him glory, his swimming skills, ended up being the cause of his tragic and ironic death.

LOL

Anthony woke up one morning with an uncontrollable urge to laugh. At first, he thought it was just a strange dream, but as he sat up in bed, the laughter continued to pour out of him. He was alarmed and scared, unsure of what was happening to him. He tried to stop laughing, but it was as if he had no control over his own body.

Desperate for help, Anthony called 911. But when the operator picked up, he found himself laughing at her, unable to speak coherently. He hung up the phone, horrified by his own behavior.

He went to the bathroom and looked at himself in the mirror. His face was contorted in a grotesque grin, his mouth open wide in laughter. But his eyes were filled with fear and confusion. His jaw ached from the tension.

Anthony knew he needed to get to the hospital. He got into his car and drove. At a red light, he looked over at the car next to him and saw the woman inside laughing at him. He thought it was just his imagination, but then he looked at the car on the other side of him and saw the driver laughing too.

As he drove to the hospital, he saw more and more people laughing on the street, as if they had all heard the funniest joke in the world. There was a line-up leading up to the emergency room, with people of all ages and seemingly healthy laughing out loud.

Anthony turned on the radio, hoping for an explanation. But instead of finding answers, he heard the host of the show laughing uncontrollably. He realized that the laughter was everywhere, that it was spreading like a virus.

As he pulled into the hospital parking lot, he didn't see the woman who walked in front of his car. He hit her violently and she lay on his bumper, laughing maniacally, in a mix of pain and hilarity. Anthony laughed along with her, understanding that there was nothing he could do to stop it. The laughing virus had taken over, and there was no cure.

The host on the radio was alerting her audience that the laughing virus was spreading worldwide. Anthony laughed harder than he ever had before, realizing that his life would now be a dark comedy.

THE COVID KILLER

In the year 2019, the world was plagued by a deadly
virus, and a hypochondriac woman named Rita was scared
of everything including this. She had heard about the
COVID Killer, a man who killed those infected with the
virus, and took every precaution to protect herself.
She installed five locks on her front door and checked
through the peephole every time she heard a noise.

One day, Rita felt the symptoms of COVID-19 and got a
rapid test at the pharmacy. But when she fainted there, she
wasn't sure if it was due to the virus or the stress. Back at
home, she did the test and it was positive. She was scared
to death of dying from the virus or the COVID Killer.

That night, Rita wrote about her infection on social
media, but immediately regretted it and deleted her
message. She didn't want to draw attention to herself
and certainly not from the COVID Killer. Suddenly, her
phone rang, and it was the pharmacist checking on her.
The pharmacist told her that the test she got might
have been part of a batch of defective tests and invited
her to come back to the pharmacy for a new one.

Rita mustered up the courage to go to the pharmacy, but when she got there, it was closed. Confused, she went back to her apartment building and took the elevator up. As she walked down the narrow hall to her apartment, she heard the elevator door open and close. She shivered and tried to find her keys, but they fell on the ground. She felt a presence behind her, but she tried to ignore it and unlocked the five locks on her door.

But as she finally opened the door, she was grabbed from behind and stung by a large syringe filled with poison. She died convulsing, as the COVID Killer pronounced the words, "Must end COVID". Rita's last words were lost in the silence of the dark, narrow hall of her apartment building, as the COVID Killer disappeared into the night, leaving behind only death and fear.

AVA

Sophie's obsession with creepypastas led her to the legend of "Ava," a reclusive woman so grotesque that looking at her was said to cause death. According to the legend, Ava never walked, instead, she crawled on the floor and walls due to her spine-less figure. It was said that she would crawl into people's houses through the chimneys at night, watching them as they slept. She had a particular fascination with toes and would stare at feet for hours on end.

One night, Sophie found herself in the perfect mood for a creepypasta and read a few, getting drunk as she often did. Later that night, she felt uneasy, like someone was watching her from outside her window. As a horror fan, she loved and fed that feeling. Sophie went to bed late, exhausted and drunk.

But when she woke up, she felt her feet were wet. Horrified, she looked down to see Ava, her grotesque, spine-less figure licking her toes. Sophie tried to scream, but no sound came out of her mouth. She was paralyzed with fear and her heart was pounding so hard she thought it would burst out of her chest.

Ava's face was distorted, twisted with a grotesque smile, her eyes were empty and her hair was tangled and greasy. Sophie noticed that Ava had long fingers with sharp nails. Sophie was so terrified that she felt her soul leaving her body and she lay there, petrified and lifeless. But Ava was not done yet, she began gnawing off Sophie's toes as she lay there, helpless and alone.

POCKET FAIRY

I had always carried my pocket fairy, an imaginary friend I had kept with me since childhood. The fairy was my constant companion, always there to protect me and shield me from harm.

As I grew older, my pocket fairy saved my life repeatedly, deflecting those who sought to harm me and bringing me good luck when I needed it most. Despite this, I never looked back and chose to forget what the fairy had done to keep me safe all my life.

One day, I reached into my pocket and found my pocket fairy dead of old age. I was filled with sadness and fear, as I realized that I had never been truly alone, and now I was. Without my pocket fairy's protection, I felt exposed and vulnerable, as if the world was closing in on me.

Questions began to haunt me: Who would love me? Who would listen to me and understand me? Who would I blame my mistakes on? Who would forgive me? Who would tell me where to hide the bodies?

THE IRON LUNG

It was 1971 and Tania Williams had always been terrified of her uncle, Roland. He was confined to an iron lung and would always stare at her, reminding her of the times he had touched her inappropriately when she was young, as well as the perverted jokes he would tell. Tania loathed him with a passion.

One day, Tania and her parents went to play golf, and when they returned, the power was out and the iron lung was off. Roland had suffocated and died. Tania's grieving father sold the iron lung to a man named Terry Davis, who used it for his own father.

Soon, Terry's father began to complain about hearing a man's voice at night, which scared him and kept him from sleeping. Terry dismissed it as his father's dementia caused by medication. In return, his father would mock Terry's new-age ways, his diets, and his vegan tendencies.

One night, Terry was awakened by the fire alarm
and found his father burning in the iron lung. He put
out the fire, but his father had already died. Days
passed, and Terry couldn't escape the memories of
his father's death. So, he moved to a new area.

A month later, Lynn Perez bought Terry's house and died in
her bed the week she moved in. Her sleep apnea machine
had become defective and stopped working during the night.
Tania Williams, Lynn's new housemaid, was deeply disturbed
when she found Lynn dead that morning. It reminded her of
her uncle's iron lung. It was as if death by asphyxiation was
following her, she thought, as she used her asthma pump.

THE TRAGIC 8 BALL

Nina had always been entranced by the ominous, black-and-white orb with its solitary, glowing window. Her curiosity about the future had always been insatiable, and so, when she stumbled upon the magic 8 ball at a garage sale, she couldn't resist its allure.

As she shook the ball and posed her first question, she was astounded by its eerie accuracy. She quickly became addicted to the magic 8 ball, relying on it to make decisions about everything from her job to her relationships.

But as she delved deeper into the magic 8 ball's predictions, she soon realized that its responses alternated between gain and loss, positive and negative. Each new prediction was more dire and impactful than the last, and she found herself unable to stop shaking the ball, no matter how much she wanted to.

One day, as she shook the ball and asked "What happens today?", the answer that appeared in the small window sent shivers down her spine. "Someone will attempt to kill you." Terrified, she rushed home and locked herself in, spending the day and evening peeking through the window, too afraid to leave. She didn't want her parents to know about the magic 8 ball, but she could see the suspicion in their eyes. Too late, she realized in horror that the killer the magic 8 ball had been referring to was none other than her own brother, who was sleepwalking with a knife in hand.

As she died by his blade, the last thing Nina saw was the magic 8 ball on her nightstand, as her brother reached out to shake it and ask his own question.

THE MUSHROOM GOD

Keith and Charles were two unsuspecting young men, who thought they had found the ultimate high in experimenting with mushrooms. But as they ingested what they believed to be magic mushrooms, they soon realized their mistake. The visions they saw were not of this world, but of a realm beyond their understanding. They saw spirits and otherworldly beings, and then, they saw the ultimate horror. The Mushroom God.

The Mushroom God appeared before them, and they were both paralyzed with fear. They couldn't believe they were actually seeing a god, let alone the god of mushrooms. They asked question after question, but the answers they received only deepened their fear. As they spoke, they began to forget that they were tripping and started to believe that this was all real.

The Mushroom God revealed to them that they had been in a mushroom-induced coma for over a year, and all the while, they had been dead. They were shocked and horrified, as they realized that they had been in this state for far longer than they had ever imagined. The god also revealed to them all the good and bad things they had done in their lives, and they were forced to confront the weight of their actions. Keith and Charles were fascinated by the discussion, but as time passed, they realized that they were trapped in a never-ending nightmare, with no way out.

As the days turned into weeks and the weeks turned into months, Charles's body began to give out. The god told Keith that Charles would soon die and that he would be left alone. Keith was devastated, but he knew he couldn't leave Charles behind. He watched in horror as Charles slowly wasted away, and as he took his last breath, Keith knew that he would be trapped in this eternal nightmare forever. He was doomed to spend eternity trapped in the realm of the Mushroom God, haunted by the visions of his past and the weight of his actions.

ORGASM

Maggie and William were inseparable friends, always seeking out new thrills and adventures. One fateful night at the club, they discovered a mysterious new street drug known only as "Orgasm." It came in a liquid form and promised to deliver the most intense climaxes imaginable. Without hesitation, they downed the drug and felt its effects almost immediately.

As the night progressed, they found themselves losing all inhibitions and becoming increasingly drawn to each other. They danced and kissed with wild abandon, unable to resist the pull of their newfound attraction. Eventually, they left the club and hailed a taxi to William's apartment, where the effects of the drug reached their peak.

They spent the night in a frenzy of unbridled passion, unable to get enough of each other. They experienced orgasms, unlike anything they had ever felt before, and were left wanting more. The next morning, they woke up still feeling incredibly aroused, and could not stop thinking about the other's touch.

As the days went by, the need for sex became all-consuming, and they found themselves unable to focus on anything else. They decided to see a doctor together and mentioned the drug, and were shocked when the doctor revealed that they both had a parasite living inside them, causing their insatiable sexual appetite. The doctor surmised that the parasite probably came from the drug and that removing it would likely kill them.

With no other options, Maggie and William ended their relationships with their partners and became a couple, the only way to keep the parasite satisfied. They were trapped in a never-ending cycle of pleasure and fear, unable to break free from the hold of the mysterious Orgasm.

THE LIE DETECTOR

Jeff Thompson, a young and ambitious police recruit, was eager to make a name for himself in the force. He had been assigned to interrogate a murder suspect named Henry, a seemingly middle-aged man who had been arrested on suspicion of murder.

As Thompson began his questioning, he made sure to hook Henry up to a lie detector to ensure the accuracy of his answers. But what he discovered was truly shocking. According to the lie detector, Henry was over 800 years old.

As Thompson looked on in disbelief, Henry began confessing to a string of crimes he had committed over the centuries. He explained that anyone who had lived as long as he had, good or bad, would eventually break the law and that he understood that jail was inevitable. But there was one thing that Henry couldn't understand: he couldn't die. He didn't know why.

Despite his shock, Thompson pressed on with the questioning. He asked Henry if he had ever killed anyone, to which Henry replied that he had killed many people and that they all deserved it. He claimed that he was guided by angels to slay evil.

As Thompson listened in horror, writing everything down, Henry began listing the names of his victims. And when Thompson asked Henry if he could currently hear the angels, Henry replied that he could and that they were telling him to "kill the interrogator."

With a sense of growing unease, Thompson got up from his chair, pulled out his gun, and ordered Henry to show his handcuffed hands. But before he could react, Henry closed his eyes and hypnotized Thompson with the power of his mind. He suggested that Thompson shoot himself in the head, and before anyone could intervene, Thompson did just that.

When the policemen outside the room heard the gunshot and saw the scene on camera, they rushed into the interrogation room. But Henry was gone. All that was left of him were a pair of handcuffs on the chair he had been sitting on. And when they looked at the footage of the interrogation, they realized that Henry had been speaking in a language they had never heard before. When they looked at Thompson's list of murder victims, it was nothing more than scribbles on the page.

CUPID LIFE

David, a struggling writer, had been searching for love for years without success. Despite his less-than-handsome appearance, he held onto the belief that he deserved to date women beyond his league, which resulted in numerous rejections. Desperate for love, he subscribed to a mysterious dating website called "Cupid Life". The site asked him an endless list of personal questions about himself, his interests, and his ideal partner. After eight days of answering these intrusive questions, David was finally matched with several women through the site. However, he was never satisfied with his matches and continued his search for the perfect woman.

One night, after a few too many drinks, David messaged the woman on the site who was least compatible with him, Cynthia. The site had only matched them with a mere 1% compatibility. Her profile was unappealing and every other word she typed in their conversations had typos, but her pictures were stunning. They exchanged a few messages and she invited him over to her apartment. Despite his reservations, David agreed, still under the influence of alcohol.

As he approached Cynthia's building, he was horrified by
its decrepit appearance. He hesitated, wondering why a
woman as gorgeous as Cynthia would live in such a place.
He entered the apartment, calling out her name, but
was met with silence. The putrid stench that filled the
air made him feel sick. Suddenly, he heard the sound of
locks clicking shut behind him, and when he turned to see
who had locked him in, a shiver went down his spine.

What he encountered was an ogre, standing far too tall
for the room and adorned with red lipstick and a wig. The
ogre hugged him and kissed him, then dragged him to the
bedroom. There, he was thrown onto a bed surrounded
by bodies piled up in the corners. The ogre began singing
a song that David hated more than anything, and he
realized with horror that the ogre was a manifestation
of all that he despised, wanting to mate with him.

THE OLD RADIO

Three boys stumbled upon an ancient radio in an abandoned house on the outskirts of their small town. Intrigued, they spent their days tuning in to its broadcasts, which seemed to be transmissions from the past. As the days passed, the year of the broadcasts progressed, and the boys were enthralled by the stories they heard.

But one day, the broadcast came from just one year before the present. The boys eagerly awaited the next day's transmission, but to their dismay, no signal came through. Despite their attempts to adjust the dials and replace the batteries, the radio remained silent.

The following day, the signal returned, but this time, it was from one year in the future. The radio host was frantic, warning listeners that World War III had erupted, sparked by a series of atomic explosions in Europe and Africa. The boys tried to alert their parents, but when they tuned in to the radio, all they could hear was a deafening static.

Desperate, the boys returned to the radio the next day, only to find it wouldn't turn on at all. They knew the end of the world was coming, but they were powerless to stop it. No one would believe their warnings of a magic radio, and so they were forced to helplessly watch as humanity was consumed by war and destruction.

THE PROMISE

I was once homeless, living on the streets and begging for money. My gambling addiction had consumed me, leaving me with nothing but despair and regret. But one day, a mysterious woman approached me. She offered me a gold necklace, but with a catch. She made me promise that I would always give money to homeless people when they begged, and in exchange, she would give me the necklace to pawn and start a new life. Desperate for a way out, I agreed to her terms.

I pawned the necklace and received $12,000, enough to get an apartment and a job. I even started going to therapy to address my addiction. For a while, I kept my promise and felt a sense of fulfillment in helping others who were in the same situation I had once been in. But as time passed, my vice crept back into my life. I started frequenting the casino more and more, and eventually, I lost it all.

One day, on my way to the casino, I was approached by a homeless person who begged for money. But I refused, telling myself that I had to save what little money I had left for the casino. That night, I got drunk and played until I lost all my money. A month later, I was back on the streets, begging for money, feeling worse than I ever had before.

I was cold and shivering, sitting on the sidewalk when the woman who had given me the necklace reappeared. A few feet away from me, she was offering the same gold necklace she had given me to an old homeless woman. Then, she looked at me with disappointment in her eyes and gave me a dollar. "You should've kept your promise," she said in a cold voice.

That night, I followed the old homeless woman to the pawn shop. In a moment of desperation and anger, I jumped her, dragged her into the alley behind the pawn shop, and stole her necklace. When I went to pawn it, the clerk, with a concerned look, went into the back room supposedly to appraise the necklace. A few minutes later, two policemen entered the pawn shop and interrogated me. They told me the necklace had been reported stolen and they arrested me. At that moment, I saw the old homeless woman enter the pawn shop, upset and crying.

The necklace was a symbol of my second chance, but as I broke my promise, I was sentenced to life in prison for my past crimes. As I sit in my cell, I can't help but think of the old homeless woman and the mysterious woman who gave me the necklace. I realize now that they were not just random strangers, but a manifestation of my conscience and a reminder of the promise I broke. And I will spend the rest of my days haunted by the memory of my mistake.

THE PIN GOBLIN

Oliver loved going to the old bowling center on weekends.
He loved the sound of the balls rolling down the alley,
the clatter of the pins falling, and the thrill of getting
a strike. But one day, something strange happened.

After throwing his ball, Oliver waited for it to come back
to him, but it didn't. He also noticed that the pins weren't
resetting themselves. Two other alleys had the same
problem. The players were confused and the owner of
the bowling center was nowhere in sight to help them.

Curious, Oliver decided to investigate. He went
through the door that led to the narrow room behind
the alleys, where the pin-setting machinery was
presumably located. What he found horrified him.

In the corner of the room, he saw the old, mythical goblin
he had heard rumors about. It was shackled and lying on
the ground. Oliver remembered the urban legend about
the pin goblin who resets the pins behind the curtain
and throws back the bowling balls to the players.

The goblin was barely breathing and it looked at
Oliver with what energy it had left. Oliver was
horrified and couldn't believe what he was seeing. He
quickly left the room, not daring to look back.

On his way out, he convinced his friends to leave
with him and they could see the terror in his eyes.
The owner of the bowling center looked at him
suspiciously, as if he knew what Oliver had seen.

Oliver never returned to the bowling alley. He couldn't shake
the image of the dying goblin from his mind, and it haunted
him for years to come. He never shared his experience
with anyone, and the bowling alley eventually closed down.
Whenever Oliver passed by the abandoned building, he could
have sworn he heard the goblin's voice pleading for release.

THE CRUISE SHIP

I met her on the first day of the cruise. Her name was Jennifer and she was the most beautiful woman I had ever seen. We hit it off right away and spent every moment of the trip together. We laughed, we danced, and we fell in love.

But one night, she went to get drinks and never returned. I searched the ship from top to bottom but there was no sign of her. Days passed and it felt like the boat would never reach its destination. Every day, the population of the cruise ship seemed to decrease. People I had seen just the day before were nowhere to be found.

I was terrified and alone. I knew something was very wrong. And then, it hit me. I was a ghost. Like Jennifer and the other passengers, I had died when the cruise ship sank. We were all trapped in an endless nightmare, doomed to relive the terror of that fateful night for eternity.

As I roamed the corridors of the ghost ship, I could
hear the screams of the dying and the wails of the
damned. The ship was in ruins, and the water was filling
the rooms, floor by floor. I could feel the cold embrace
of the ocean, but my body was not there to feel it.

I looked for Jennifer everywhere but all I found were the
remnants of the tragic event, the broken glasses, the spilled
drinks, and the last messages on the cell phones. My heart
ached with longing and sorrow, knowing that I would never
be able to hold her again, to tell her how much I loved her.

I was trapped in this ghost ship, alone with my thoughts and
regrets, forever searching for her, but never finding her.
I should have never boarded that ship, and I should have
never fallen in love with Jennifer. But now, it's too late.
Now, I am doomed to wander the ghost ship alone, forever.

THE LAST PARADOX

Martin was a practitioner of the occult, but he
had never fully believed in the legends and myths
surrounding it. That was until one day when he began
to see a distortion in his vision. At first, he questioned
his eyesight, but then he saw a magician.

The magician was dressed in purple, wearing a trench coat and
a crown, and holding what appeared to be a magic staff. His
whole being was flickering, and Martin remembered the legend
of Dreen, the shapeshifting magician who erases paradoxes.

Supposedly, when you see the magician, you soon forget
having seen him as he erases whatever paradox he came for.
According to legend, paradoxes occur when two dimensions
merge by accident or when they are tampered with.

Martin watched as the magician walked towards a nervous
man who was repeatedly shouting "he's real!" The man began
to run from him, but the magician, surrounded by lightning,
turned into a tall ethereal creature and cast a portal
that engulfed the man. The magician then disappeared.

A week later, Martin was surprised to even remember this encounter. As he was coming back from an occult shop, he saw the magician again on the site of an accident involving two cars. His vision became distorted again and flickered. The cars were the same model and color.

As Martin approached the scene, he saw from a distance that the two drivers looked similar and wore the same clothes. The magician shapeshifted into its spirit form and erased both cars with a magic spell. Both cars and drivers disappeared. The crowd surrounding the car seemed to forget all about it and resumed their day as if they hadn't noticed anything strange.

One morning, as he woke up and looked through the window of his bedroom, Martin saw the magician walking towards his porch. He fled his house through the patio door, running as fast as he could. He thought he had evaded him and came back home to pack his things and leave. He planned on spending a few days at his girlfriend's. He called her to tell her about it.

When he arrived at her apartment and knocked, he could hear his girlfriend's muffled voice through the door and another voice. A man's voice. The man opened the door. Martin, horrified, saw a copy of himself in front of him. He then understood the magician's purpose - to eliminate all paradoxes. He and his doppelganger were paradoxes, Martin thought, as the elevator door opened and the magician came out, holding his staff, flickering, and moving towards them.

Martin knew why the magician was after him. The last thought he had, that day, was that he shouldn't have tried that conjuration spell a week before. He wasn't sure he truly believed in the occult before that day, and he didn't know how to revert his magic spell, but the magician knew exactly how. And with that, Martin and his doppelganger were erased from existence, leaving no paradox behind.

ROUGH NEIGHBORHOOD

As I walk home, I feel the crushing weight of depression. The world around me seems to be closing in and I can't escape the darkness that engulfs me. People avoid my gaze as if they can sense the darkness within me, only confirming my suspicions. I haven't been doing the things I used to love, like dancing, and I've been feeling really down lately. I'm not sleeping well and I've been eating a lot, but I still feel too skinny, as if I can't gain weight.

I've been getting into arguments more often and I know I can be rough and impatient with others. I try to blend in as I walk through my neighborhood, hoping to avoid attracting any invasive neighbors, but the truth is, I don't care. The constant turmoil in my mind is only exacerbated by the gunshots and screams I hear at night.

When I reach my home, I stand before the living room mirror. My eyes blaze with a malevolent red glow and my skin is torn and tattered, evidence of the atrocities I have committed. I can't remember how I got here or even where "here" is. The shattered front door and the trail of blood leading to my feet paint a horrifying picture. Then, it all rushes back to me, like a cruel joke played by fate. I am a zombie, cursed to roam the earth and consume all that crosses my path. But the cruelest twist of all? I forget, time and time again, that I am dead.

FIVE STARS

It had been several months since my girlfriend went missing without a trace. The police had no leads and I was left with nothing but grief and a constant feeling of emptiness.

As a film critic, I received a mysterious package in the mail one day. Inside was a screener copy of an upcoming film, but something about it felt off. The movie was dark and disturbing, depicting acts of violence and torture that made me feel sick to my stomach.

As the movie progressed, it felt like I was watching something real, something that was actually happening. And then, in the final segment of the film, I saw her. My girlfriend, tied up and being brutally murdered on camera.

I was in shock, unable to process what I had just seen. I immediately called the police and reported what I had witnessed, but the investigation dragged on.

I became consumed by anger and a desire for revenge. I spent every waking moment trying to track down the person or people responsible for this sick and twisted snuff film.

One day, I woke up dizzy and disoriented, tied to a workshop table naked. When I saw the camera filming me, I understood that I was the next victim. That someone, somewhere, would watch my demise and maybe even give it a five-star rating.

THE MAN ON THE TAPES

Naomi had always found comfort in revisiting her childhood through her collection of VHS tapes. But one night, as she sat in front of the TV, something caught her eye that sent shivers down her spine. In the background of the footage, she noticed a man lurking, always watching her from a distance. At first, she thought it was her imagination playing tricks on her, but as she continued to watch the tapes, the man's presence became undeniable.

Naomi delved deeper into the footage, searching for closer shots of the man. To her horror, she realized that it was her boyfriend, Mason. However, the footage was over thirty years old, yet Mason appeared to be the same age as he was now, which was impossible. Memories flooded back to Naomi of how Mason always seemed to know her better than she knew herself and how controlling he had become in recent months, always insisting on knowing her plans and whereabouts.

That night, when Mason returned home, Naomi quickly turned off the TV, but it was too late. Mason asked her what she had been watching and she answered "nothing". He then replied with a low, accusatory voice, "You found out, didn't you."

Naomi's heart raced as she backed away from Mason. He began to move towards her, and she grabbed a knife from the kitchen counter. "I can explain," he said, but before he could, Naomi defended herself by stabbing him. He fell to the floor, bleeding out.

As he lay dying, Mason whispered, "I was your protector, always have been. You were destined to change the world, but now you'll have to do it on your own." And with those final words, his body turned to sand and collapsed on the floor.

Naomi was left alone with her thoughts, staring at a model spaceship that was a reminder of her upcoming astronaut mission. She wondered what Mason had been protecting her from and what could be waiting for her in space. Maybe something that had been waiting for her for a long time. The thought of it all filled her with dread and uncertainty, but she knew that she had to face it, alone.

ETERNITY BRIDGE

The man was driving through the small town of Eternity
for the first time when his car broke down. He had
heard rumors of the town being cursed but shrugged
them off as nothing more than superstition. He didn't
have a signal on his phone, so he decided to walk
to the nearest gas station, hoping to find help.

As he walked, a thick fog rolled in, obscuring his vision
and making it difficult to navigate. He had been walking
for an hour and still couldn't see the end of the bridge
he was on. He began to feel uneasy as if the bridge was
never-ending. He wondered if he was dreaming, knowing
full well he wasn't but looking for an explanation.

He decided to turn back and retrace his steps, but after
two hours of walking, he still hadn't reached the end of
the bridge. The fog had grown denser and the darkness was
closing in around him. He was starting to feel trapped.

He couldn't take it anymore. He had been walking for over an hour in this direction. He was overcome with a sense of hopelessness and despair. He climbed over the railing and jumped off the bridge, falling into the darkness below.

As he fell, he realized that the rumors were true. The town of Eternity was cursed, and he was now trapped in an endless cycle of falling, forever. He screamed and cried out, but no one could hear him. He was doomed to fall for all eternity, a prisoner of the bridge.

To this day, some say that on a foggy night, you can still hear the screams of the man echoing through the streets of Eternity. Beware, for if you ever find yourself stranded in this cursed town, you may never find your way out.

DR. GASLIGHT

For eight long years, I've been visiting my psychiatrist on a monthly basis. At first, I thought he was my savior, understanding my troubles and always having the right words to ease my pain. But as time passed, something began to feel off. It was as if he knew my thoughts before I even spoke them. As if he were reading my mind.

Doubt and suspicion crept into my mind. I felt manipulated, gaslighted. I couldn't trust him anymore. But when he requested an appointment the following week, I didn't question it.

The next appointment was different. I was agitated, and my psychiatrist had me committed to a psychiatric hospital. I spent the night there, and the next day, I met with him in one of the hospital's offices. I demanded to know why I had been brought in the day before. But what he told me was beyond horrifying.

He revealed that I had been committed and locked in this hospital for the last eight years and that I had been seeing him every month since, yet there had been no improvement in my mental health. He informed me that I would be relocated to a new facility and that this was our last appointment.

I couldn't comprehend the reality of the situation. Eight years of my life, stolen from me without my knowledge. Had my mind been so manipulated that I had forgotten? My mind raced as I struggled to grasp the concept of time. What day was it? What was my name?

THE EXTRA

There was once a man who had a peculiar fetish. He would visit a brothel where all the clients were required to be blindfolded at all times. The brothel specialized in erotic massages, and the man had found his favorite masseuse. She was always gentle, and always gave him the "extra" that he craved. He would leave the brothel feeling satisfied and relaxed.

But one day, as he was getting "the extra" from his usual masseuse, he couldn't resist the temptation any longer and removed his blindfold as he orgasmed. What he saw was something that he could never have imagined.

It looked like an alien, with a machine that looked otherworldly. The alien had some sort of tube that was attached to the man's genitals, and it was absorbing his sperm with the machine. The man was horrified, and the alien noticed that he had removed his blindfold. The alien threatened the man that his race would hunt him down if he ever told anyone what the "extra" was all about.

The man was so scared that he never had sex again. He could never forget the image of the alien and the machine, and the thought of it still haunts him to this day.

FORTUNE

Jill had always been skeptical of fortune tellers, but she couldn't deny the accuracy of the predictions made by the mysterious woman she met at a convention the month before. Everything the fortune teller had predicted had come true - her promotion at work, her unexpected inheritance, and even her newfound love. So when Jill found herself at an amusement park and saw the same fortune teller's tent set up among the attractions, she couldn't resist paying for another reading.

As she sat across from the woman, she noticed a hint of fear in her eyes. The fortune teller took her hand, and with a tremble in her voice, she delivered her prediction: "You will die by the end of the day unless you fight your fate with what you know."

Jill was shocked and couldn't believe what she was hearing. She quickly left the tent and walked through the amusement park, feeling disoriented. Everywhere she went, she had close calls - almost getting hit by a malfunctioning ride, almost falling down a stairway, and almost being burned by a fire-breather.

She knew she had to get home, where it was safe. She hesitated for a long time before finally taking her car. She was careful driving home, but she couldn't avoid the other car that crashed into her. The impact was deadly, and the last thing she saw before she died was the bleeding face of the fortune teller, in the other car, looking just as surprised as she was.

THE LONG GAME

Zoe and Anna had always been close friends, and when they stumbled upon an old board game at a garage sale, they knew they had to have it. The game was called "Determination," and it promised hours of fun and excitement.

They set up the game on the kitchen table, and as the night went on, they drank energy drinks and ate coffee beans to stay awake. They were determined to finish the game, no matter how long it took.

After 15 hours of play, Zoe and Anna began to feel the effects of fatigue. Anna lay down on the couch in the living room to take a break, while Zoe finished her turn. She drew a card she had never seen before. The card simply said, "You win. Start over."

Excited and exhausted, Zoe went to check on Anna in the living room. But she wasn't there. Zoe searched the whole house, calling out her name, but there was no answer. Her car was still parked outside. She tried calling Anna's phone, but there was no answer.

Panic set in as Zoe returned to the kitchen table, and she saw that the board game had reset itself. All the pieces were back in their starting positions. That's when she noticed something strange. There was a game miniature on the board that she had never seen before. As she looked closer, she recognized Anna's clothes and baseball cap. The miniature was made of resin, and it was a perfect replica of her friend, who looked horrified as if she was still very much alive.

Zoe kept the game locked away and never talked about it. She hoped to find the courage to play again with a new person, someone she wouldn't mind sacrificing, hoping to free Anna from her resin prison.

NECROFIX

Target, a skilled hitman, had been hired to take out Necrofix, a powerful necromancer rumored to reside deep in the heart of the mountains. Despite the vague information provided by the locals, Target set out on his mission, determined to find and eliminate his mark at any cost.

As he hiked through the rugged terrain, he finally spotted the small pyramid that was said to be Necrofix's lair. The pyramid loomed over the landscape, its ominous presence filling Target with a sense of unease. But he pressed on, determined to complete his mission.

As he approached the stone doors of the pyramid, they suddenly closed behind him, trapping him inside with the powerful necromancer. Necrofix emerged from the shadows, unleashing a bone-crushing magic spell upon Target. But Target was quick on his feet, and he managed to shoot Necrofix with his silenced pistol.

To his surprise, Necrofix's body collapsed, but another version of him appeared from an adjacent room, stabbing Target in the process with a twisted, rusty knife. Target quickly shot this new Necrofix, but the same thing happened again and again. Each time Target killed one version of the necromancer, another would spawn elsewhere, each one more twisted and evil than the last.

With no other options, Target decided to enter the adjacent room where Necrofix had been spawning from. Inside, he found a chalk pentacle on the floor with a copy of Necrofix floating above it. He quickly killed the necromancer and erased the pentacle, putting an end to the spawning cycle.

But as he turned to leave, the stone doors of the barely-lit room shut themselves, trapping him inside with a dozen pentacles, each with a copy of Necrofix floating over them. Target realized in horror that he was a prisoner of a room with no way out, and with no way to stop the spawning of Necrofix. He was out of luck and out of bullets, and with no way out, Target knew his fate was sealed.

HARVESTER

Tommy walked alone in a dark alley, feeling the effects of the alcohol he had consumed at the tavern. He stumbled and nearly fell, but caught himself on a nearby wall. As he looked up, he saw a figure approaching him. It was a man, dressed in black, with a hood covering his face. He carried a scythe and had an aura of death around him. Tommy was frozen with fear, he couldn't move, speak or even scream. He knew who the figure was, it was Harvester, the grim reaper.

Harvester stood in front of Tommy and spoke in a deep and ominous voice. "Tommy, you have lived your life with recklessness and disregard for the people around you, and now it's time to face the consequences." Tommy tried to speak, to defend himself, but the spell kept him silent. Harvester continued, "I will give you one chance, to make amends for your actions. What, in life, would you do differently?"

Tommy struggled to find an answer, fighting the spell and the alcohol. He knew deep down that he had made many mistakes in his life. He had hurt a lot of people, lost the love of his life, and wasted his talents. He admitted that he should have never touched a drop of alcohol and that enough people suffered for it. He realized that his addiction had blinded him to the pain and suffering of others, and he wished he could go back in time and change it.

The reaper listened to his answer, and then he removed the spell that paralyzed Tommy. He let him go, with a warning. "I will be watching you, Tommy. If you ever touch alcohol again, I will come back for you, and there will be no second chance." Tommy nodded, terrified by the thought of Harvester's return.

From that moment on, alcohol meant demise to Tommy. Every time he even thought of drinking, he swore he could see the reaper in the corner of his eye. He knew that Harvester was watching him, and he didn't want to disappoint him. Tommy lived sober, and he tried to make amends for his past actions.

But as the years passed, Tommy grew older and more depressed. He couldn't shake the memory of the reaper, and the weight of his past mistakes weighed heavily on him. He became increasingly isolated and disconnected from the world around him.

One day, unable to bear the thought of living with the guilt and shame of his past any longer, Tommy decided to end it all. He returned to the tavern where he had first met the reaper and got drunk like he never had before. He knew that by doing so, he was inviting Harvester to come for him, and he wanted him to.

The next morning, Tommy was found dead in the alley behind the tavern, the victim of alcohol poisoning.

HORRIFIED

I was thrilled when I first heard about the new social horror game, "Horrified." It promised to scare players when they least expected it, through phone, email, or social media. I eagerly subscribed, ready for the thrill of the unknown.

But things quickly took a dark turn. The game began to extort me, threatening to reveal private information to the world. It sent me videos of me cheating on my girlfriend, taken from my bedroom webcam. I was terrified and infuriated.

I decided to investigate the creators of the game online, but at first, I found no information. After hours of research, I stumbled upon an address: 741 Clark Street. Without hesitation, I drove to the location, eager to confront the people behind the game.

But when I arrived, I couldn't find the number 741. I walked around and between the two buildings where my destination should've been, but still couldn't find it. As I returned to my car, I found pictures on the driver's seat. I was convinced that I had locked the door and wondered how someone got in.

The pictures showed me purchasing illegal drugs from my drug dealer. And then I saw a mysterious figure watching me, filming me with a camera, and walking away. I followed him with my car, but he started to run as I got closer. Fueled by rage, I got out of my car and chased him down, beating him brutally behind a dumpster.

But as I left the scene, I realized that I couldn't see clearly anymore. When I got home, my knuckles were raw and bleeding, I opened a beer and tuned in to the local news. But on the television, I saw a clip of myself brutally attacking the man. My face was visible.

The heavy knocking on my front door was like a death knell. As I peered through the peephole, an army of police officers stood before me, a warrant for my arrest in hand. The last image that seared into my mind before being dragged away in handcuffs was that of the pictures the man had taken of me, being broadcast on the news as evidence that would incriminate me as the killer in the eyes of the authorities. My life, my reputation, and my freedom were all ruined in an instant. I was consumed with a sense of hopelessness and despair as I was led away to face the consequences of my actions.

One night, while in jail, a guard dropped a mobile phone into my cell containing instructions for a new game. The thought of it haunted me, and it made me paranoid, but what else was I to do with the rest of my life, trapped within these walls? I played the game and I excelled at it.

2:22

The students of the college were living in fear. Every Friday at 2:22 PM, one of their own would suddenly combust and die. Rumors of a mysterious pyromaniac spread, but no one could figure out how the fires were starting. The school closed for a month, but when classes resumed, the fires started again.

Debbie, who had lost five friends this way, noticed something strange. Every new victim had been romantically involved with the previous one. She was worried that her turn would come, as the recent victims were in her circle of friends. When Debbie's friend Isabelle went up in flames, at 2:22 PM in the hallway, Debbie understood how the curse contaminates. It was a sexually transmitted disease. Isabelle was dead and so was her ex and the woman he had sex with that month they took a break.

When Debbie told her theory to her boyfriend Oscar, who was mourning his ex-girlfriend Isabelle, he froze and seemed in shock. It also made sense to him: the disease was moving from body to body and combusting a chain of sexual partners. They both knew this meant Oscar might be next and after that Debbie would soon follow.

The next day, at exactly 2:22 PM, Oscar's body burst into flames in front of Debbie's eyes. She watched in horror as her boyfriend was consumed by the curse, leaving nothing but ashes behind. She knew that it was only a matter of time before it was her turn, and she began to mentally prepare for her own death. The curse had claimed yet another victim, and there was no escape from its deadly grasp. The students of the college were left with nothing but fear and dread, knowing that at any moment, they could be next.

THE KILLER'S PROFILE

Julie had always been drawn to the macabre world of true crime, particularly serial killers. So, when she decided to write an essay on the topic, she knew she had to focus on the most recent and most terrifying killer of them all: the E-Killer. He was the man who preyed on innocent victims through a popular dating app, luring them to their deaths and then cutting off their faces to use as masks to scare his next victims.

As she delved deeper into her research, Julie made the bold decision to join the dating app herself, in hopes of getting a better understanding of the E-Killer's tactics and victims. She created a profile and started browsing through the app, scanning for any sign of the killer.

At first, nothing seemed out of the ordinary. She talked to a few men, but none of them raised any red flags. But then, late one night, she received a message from a man with no pictures on his profile. He was polite and charming, and they struck up a conversation. As they talked, Julie felt something was off about him.

Finally, she asked him for a picture. He hesitated for a moment, but then sent her a photo. It was a picture of a man wearing someone else's face, and holding a knife. Behind him, she could recognize her own apartment door. At that very moment, she heard someone knocking at her door.

THE CLOWN CONVENTION

It was a typical day for Owen, an inexperienced clown, as he made his way to the annual clown convention. The excitement of meeting other clowns, buying new props and accessories, and participating in the never-ending pranks filled his heart. But little did he know that this convention would change his life forever.

As the night fell, the hotel was filled with the sound of laughter and revelry. Owen was in the bathroom texting his girlfriend when he suddenly heard a violent argument between two clowns. Curiosity got the better of him, and he peeked through the crack of his stall to see the argument. What he saw next, he could never forget.

One of the clowns transformed into a monster with a large mouth, devouring the other clown in just three bites. Owen recognized the monster as Chuckles, one of the convention's organizers. Suddenly, Owen's automatic toilet flushed, alerting Chuckles to his presence. The monster approached his stall, tearing the door off and revealing Owen's hiding spot.

Just then, three other clowns walked into the bathroom, chatting loudly. Chuckles transformed back into his human form, joked with the clowns, and left the washroom. Owen was left stunned and terrified, unable to process what he had just witnessed.

That night, Owen quit his job as a clown, haunted by the memory of Chuckles. He became afraid of clowns and could no longer perform as one. But a year later, he received a letter in the mail, an invitation to the clown convention. It was signed by none other than Chuckles.

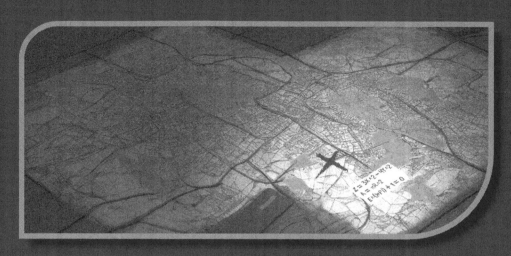

THE TREASURE MAP

Charlotte and Natalie were two teenage girls who lived in
a small town. One day, while walking home from school,
Charlotte found a crumpled treasure map on the sidewalk.
Excited by the possibility of adventure, she immediately invited
her friend Natalie to come play with her, but Natalie refused,
finding the idea juvenile and saying she had homework to do.

Undeterred, Charlotte set off on her own, determined
to solve the three equations on the map. After an
hour of work, she finally arrived at a combination that
seemed to be the answer. Eagerly, she got in her car
and drove to the location marked with an X on the
map, an abandoned farm on the outskirts of town.

In the barn, marked with an X, Charlotte found a safe. With
shaking hands, she successfully opened it with the combination
from the equations. Inside, she found a key and a note with
directions to a storage building in the city and a storage room
number. Excited and curious, Charlotte set off for the city.

Upon arriving at the storage building, Charlotte found the storage room number mentioned on the note and unlocked it with the key from the safe. She felt a sense of excitement and fear as she opened the door, unsure of what she would find inside. As she stepped into the room, her heart sank. Inside the room, she found only one object, a torture chair. It was a gruesome sight, with straps and chains attached to it, and dark stains on the seat and armrests. Suddenly, she felt a hand grasp her from behind and a cloth pressed over her nose and mouth. She struggled against the person, but it was no use. She felt herself being sedated with chloroform. The last thing she saw before losing consciousness was the empty torture chair looming in front of her. Charlotte was never seen again.

A week later, Natalie, worried about her friend's disappearance, received a letter in the mail with a map inside, marked with an X and three equations.

THE IRRITABLE GIANT

The village at the base of the mountain was plagued by a giant who would visit once every 15 years. The villagers lived in fear, knowing to keep their noise to a minimum and never cook food to avoid attracting him. They subsisted on raw food alone, and avoided going near the giant's house at all costs.

Tom, a young boy of 10, had never seen the giant but had heard of a legend that said his water could cure any illness. His grandfather was dying, and he was desperate to find a cure. He set out on a journey to the giant's house, climbing the mountain and finally arriving at his house. To his surprise, it was not the terrifying place he had imagined, but a colorful and beautiful place, with paintings and tapestries. He found the fountain and filled his water bottle with the bright blue water. But as he was about to leave, he heard the giant returning home.

Tom froze in fear as the giant entered the house, but he was soon found by him. The giant looked down at him with a fierce expression, but Tom offered him a deal. He promised to return to him and keep him company, to tell him jokes and dance for him, in exchange for letting him bring the water back to his grandfather. The giant accepted, and Tom brought the water back to the village.

But his grandfather had already passed away, and Tom was consumed by overwhelming sadness and guilt. He had lost his grandfather and his freedom all for a false hope. He knew he had to keep his promise to the giant and returned to his house, his heart heavy with dread.

Tom knew that his days were numbered. He knew that as he aged, he would eventually run out of jokes and would no longer be able to dance. He knew that once he could no longer entertain the giant, he would have no use for him and would eat him. Despite this looming fate, he continued to dance and tell jokes every day to the giant, cherishing the few good years he had left.

RAVENSWOOD'S SCARECROW

In the small farming community of Ravenswood, there is a legend of a mysterious scarecrow that only appears to those alone. This scarecrow is not like any other, for it appears and disappears in the blink of an eye. Each time the observer blinks, the scarecrow seems to change location a few feet away, as if it were playing a twisted game of hide and seek.

According to the legend, if the observer blinks ten times in the presence of the scarecrow, they will die, and their body will be taken over by its spirit. They will then continue to haunt the fields, forever seeking out new victims to replace them. But the legend does not end here, for it is said that the scarecrow is not just a mere figment of imagination, but a real entity that is as old as the community itself.

If you ever visit Ravenswood and see the scarecrow, do not blink at all, and try to leave the area as soon as possible, for you may stay there much longer than you expected.

PLUNGE TO PERDITION

The elevator in an old office building was a portal to the unknown. It was an enigma that always descended, no matter the button pressed. Those who entered never returned, as if the narrow elevator was a passage to another realm where there was no escape.

Employees had tried every possible means to halt the elevator's descent, from wrenching open the doors to cutting off power to the entire building, but all efforts were in vain. The elevator would always descend, and no one knew where it led.

On the eve of a holiday, a new employee, fueled by curiosity and alcohol, decided to take a ride. He pressed the button for the ground floor, and the elevator began to plummet at an alarming speed, plunging the employee into darkness. He tried to open the doors, but they wouldn't budge. He banged on the walls and screamed for help, but no one answered. The elevator continued its descent until it finally came to a stop.

The doors opened to a dark, underground chamber. The employee stepped out, but he was trapped. The elevator had vanished, and there was no way out. He is still, today, waiting for the elevator to reappear, hoping another reckless employee takes the haunted elevator.

It is said that anyone who comes across this elevator should not enter it, or they will be doomed to a fate worse than death. Beware of the elevator that always goes down.

THE SHRINKING ROOM

It all started one night as Erica lay in bed, trying to fall asleep. Suddenly, she noticed that the door and windows in her room had disappeared as if they were just a continuation of the walls. A sense of paralysis washed over her, and she couldn't move. But somehow, she fought through it and returned to her body. And just as quickly as it had happened, her room returned to normal.

The next night, as she lay in bed again, she experienced the same thing. But this time, it was as if the room was slowly shrinking. She felt trapped and claustrophobic, but once again, she fought through the paralysis and returned to her body. And just like before, her room returned to normal.

But the third night was different. As she lay in bed, the room without windows or walls started to shrink. This time, she couldn't move or wake up in time. She was completely paralyzed and couldn't scream for help. She couldn't even cry out in terror as the walls crept closer and closer. She knew that this was the end, and there was nothing she could do to stop it. She couldn't even pray. She was trapped, alone, and terrified as the walls crushed her, taking her life with them.

Her parents didn't find her in her bed that morning or at the breakfast table. Her body was gone, but she was very much alive, trapped within the walls, listening to her parents mourn, unable to comfort them. She was doomed to spend eternity in the walls, a prisoner in her own house.

THE JEALOUS SPIRIT

I spent most of my days on dating websites, swiping through profiles, and messaging potential matches. I was desperate for companionship and willing to overlook any red flags. That's how I ended up on a date with Lola. She was not my type at all, but I went through with it anyway.

The date was a disaster. I couldn't stand being around her, and as soon as it was over, I knew I would never speak to her again. But the next day, I saw a news story online about a woman who had committed suicide. It was Lola. I felt a pit in my stomach as I realized that my rejection of her may have played a role in her decision to take her own life.

That night, I was lying in bed when I heard a knock on my window. I got up to see what it was, but there was no one there. I shrugged it off and went back to bed. But the knocking persisted, growing louder and more frantic. I opened the window to find the ghost of Lola staring back at me. She was screaming and reaching out to me, her face twisted in pain and desperation.

From that night on, Lola's ghost haunted me everywhere I went. She followed me to work, to the grocery store, to the mall. Everywhere I looked, she was there, her eyes begging for my attention. I tried to ignore her, but it was impossible. She was always there, always watching me.

As the days went by, my dating life became a nightmare. Every woman I went on a date with died suddenly and tragically. Some of them died in accidents, others committed suicide. It was as if Lola's ghost was punishing me for my rejection of her.

One day, I was talking to my ex-wife on the phone when she suddenly screamed and then stopped responding. I called her name, but there was no answer. I panicked and called 911, but by the time they arrived at her house, she was already dead.

I couldn't take it anymore. I moved out of the city and into the countryside, becoming a hermit. I slowly lost my mind, but at least I wasn't alone. Lola's ghost was always there with me, her presence the only comfort I had left.

FORGOTTEN MEMORIES

Courtney awoke each morning with a sense of dread, her husband filling in the gaps of her forgotten memories. She knew she had a contagious mental illness that only affected women, causing memories to slowly slip away until death. She was 12 weeks pregnant and she knew she was in no condition to give birth.

She kept a journal and notes to remind herself of what she had forgotten, but it was becoming increasingly difficult to maintain. Though her physical health remained intact, her mental state was rapidly deteriorating. News reports of the disease spreading among women and the rising death toll added to her fear and desperation.

One night, Courtney read through her journal, and a sentence caught her eye, repeated over and over: "It's not contagious. The disease is in your head." She saw the word "dementia" written with increasing aggression. And on the last pages, written in big bold letters, "You are not pregnant". She walked to the mirror, looking at herself, she saw a woman that looked twice her age, wrinkles and tired eyes.

The journal revealed the truth: her dementia and memory loss had manifested as a false belief of a contagious disease. Her husband had known all along, but she couldn't bring herself to listen, consumed by her own delusions.

Her condition was not curable and would only worsen. She would continue to forget the people and things she loved, including the child that never existed. The disease was not contagious, it was the product of her own mind and it had already claimed her.

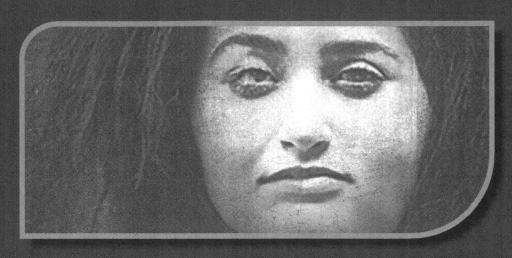

A FAMILIAR FACE

There is a viral picture of a woman circulating the internet. At first, it seems like any other picture, but as more and more people see it, they feel they have met her before. They can't remember when or where, but the feeling is undeniable.

As the picture spreads, more and more people claim to recognize the woman. Some even say they have dreamed about her. The woman in the picture is young, with long dark hair and a small smile on her lips. She seems familiar to everyone who sees her, but no one can place her.

Rumors begin to spread that the woman in the picture is some kind of ghost or spirit, haunting the internet. People start to avoid looking at the picture, afraid that it will bring bad luck or worse.

But for some, the feeling of familiarity is too strong. They can't stop thinking about the woman in the picture, trying to remember where they met her.

One day, a man claims that he has finally remembered where he has seen the woman. He says that he met her at a party, years ago. He says that she was quiet and that he barely spoke to her. But he remembers her face, and he knows that she is the woman in the viral picture.

The man's story sparks a renewed interest in the picture, and people begin to dig deeper, trying to find out who the woman is. But as they search, they find nothing. No records of her existence, no trace of her online or in real life. She is a mystery, a ghost haunting the internet.

And so, the picture of the woman remains, circulating the internet, and her story continues to be told. Some say that she is a spirit, wandering the digital realm, searching for someone to remember her. Others say that she is a curse, a reminder of something best left forgotten. But one thing is certain, anyone who sees her picture will never forget the feeling of familiarity, and the nagging suspicion that they have met her before, even though they can't remember where or when.

THE THING IN THE WOODS

Deep in the heart of the mountains, there lies a house that has stood for centuries. It is an old, decrepit structure, with boarded-up windows and a door that hangs off its hinges. But what lurks within is far more terrifying than the state of the house itself.

For years, locals have spoken of a creature that lives in the mountains and fiercely protects the old house. It is a being with two pairs of legs, a torso, and no head or arms. It runs swiftly and silently, its only purpose to terrorize anyone who dares to step into its territory.

The creature has been seen in drawings and photographs dating back to the 1920s. It is said to be one-half of Siamese twins, searching for its other half to complete itself. Some say that it is the ghost of a long-dead twin, forever searching for its lost sibling.

Those who have encountered the creature say that it is a terrifying sight to behold. It moves with a speed and agility that belies its grotesque appearance, and its silent pursuit sends chills down the spine of even the bravest of souls.

Many have tried to enter the old house, but none have returned. Those who have ventured too close to the creature have been met with a terrifying sight: the creature running towards them, its legs pounding the ground with a deafening roar, its empty torso looming larger and larger as it closes in on its prey.

Some say that the creature is a curse, placed upon the house by a vengeful witch. Others believe that it is a demon, summoned from the depths of hell to protect the house and its secrets. But whatever the truth may be, one thing is certain: the creature of the mountains is a force to be reckoned with and should be avoided at all costs.

CREEPYPASTAS REVIEWED

CREEPYPASTAS ARE A MIX OF CAMPFIRE TALES AND URBAN LEGENDS THAT HAVE EMERGED ON THE INTERNET AT THE TURN OF THE MILLENNIUM. THEY ARE THE HORROR MEMES OF A GENERATION. THEY ARE SOME OF THE EERIEST SHORT STORIES THERE ARE.

HORROR CRITIC STEVE HUTCHISON REVIEWS 93 SHORT FILMS, FEATURE FILMS, AND TELEVISION SEASONS BASED ON 28 CREEPYPASTAS (SLENDER MAN, CANDLE COVE, NO-END HOUSE, MOMO, SEARCH AND RESCUE, THE PORTRAITS, SIRED HEAD, TED THE CAVER, THE SMILING MAN, THE EXPRESSIONLESS, ROBERT THE DOLL, SUGGESTION BOX, JEFF THE KILLER, THE HIDDEN DOOR, SMILE DOG, PALE LUNA, A STORY TO SCARE MY SON, BOX FORT, THE GIRL IN THE PHOTOGRAPH, WHITE WITH RED, MOTHER'S CALL, THE RAKE, SONIC.EXE, EYELESS JACK, THE BLINK MAN, THE THING THAT STALKS THE FIELDS, THE RUSSIAN SLEEP EXPERIMENT, AND WHERE BAD KIDS GO).

TERROR.CA/BOOKS

SLENDER MAN REVIEWED

SLENDER MAN, THE ULTIMATE CREEPYPASTA, IS WHAT KEPT A GENERATION OF CHILDREN AND TEENAGERS UP AT NIGHT. HE'S THIN, UNNATURALLY TALL, WEARS A BLACK SUIT, AND HAS NO FACE. HE LIVES IN THE WOODS WHERE HE ABDUCTS THOSE WHO MEDDLE. BY HIS MYSTERIOUS NATURE, HE BECAME ONE OF THE CREEPIEST HORROR ICONS FOLLOWING HIS CREATION IN 2009.

HORROR CRITIC STEVE HUTCHISON ANALYZES 40 SLENDER MAN FEATURE FILMS AND SHORT FILMS. EACH ARTICLE INCLUDES A SYNOPSIS, FIVE RATINGS, AND A REVIEW.

TERROR.CA/BOOKS